Captain Russy

written by Jay Dale

illustrated by Tammie Lyon

Engage Literacy is published in 2013 by Raintree.
Raintree is an imprint of Capstone Global Library Limited, a company
incorporated in Engand and Wales having its registered office at 7 Pilgrim
Street, London, EC4V 6LB – Registered company number: 6695582
www.raintreepublishers.co.uk

Originally published in Australia by Hinkler Education, a division
of Hinkler Books Pty Ltd.
Text copyright © UpLoad Publishing Pty Ltd 2012
Illustration copyright © Hinkler Books Pty Ltd 2012

Written by Jay Dale
Lead authors Jay Dale and Anne Giulieri
Cover illustration and illustrations by Tammie Lyon
Edited by Gwenda Smyth
UK edition edited by Dan Nunn, Catherine Veitch and Sian Smith
Designed by Susannah Low, Butterflyrocket Design

Captain Russy
ISBN: 978 1 406 26508 8
10 9 8 7 6 5 4 3 2 1

Printed in India.

Contents

Chapter 1
Where Is Russy?

"Where is Russy?" cried Carla, as she peered into her backpack.
"Where is my teddy?"

Nana looked in Carla's bag.
She took all Carla's things out, one by one.

"I'm sorry, Carla," she said, when everything was on the bed.
"Russy's not here and he's not
in the car either.
You must have left him on the plane."

Carla had just arrived at her nana's house
for the school holidays.
She had travelled all by herself
on a large plane.
A flight attendant had looked after her
most of the way.

Russy, her special teddy,
had sat beside Carla on the plane.
But now, he was nowhere to be found.

"Oh, no!" cried Carla.
"I will never, ever see Russy again.
Some other boy or girl will find him
and keep him."
And with that, she burst into tears.

Nana gave Carla a big hug.
"I will ring the airport right now," she said,
"and see if Russy has been handed in.
Somebody may have found him."

Chapter 2
Sleep Well

While Nana spoke to a man at the airport,
Carla thought about her teddy.
Poor Russy! He would be all alone.
Nana had given Russy to Carla
when she was only two years old.
He was her very special teddy
and even though she was older now,
she still loved to cuddle him every night.

At last, Nana put her phone down.
Her face looked sad.
"I'm sorry, Carla," she said,
"but Russy has not been handed in.
The man at the airport told me to ring back
in the morning.
He said he would find out where the plane
was going, and ask the flight attendants
if they had seen Russy."

Carla felt very sad.
She missed Russy.

That night, as Carla got ready for bed,
Nana came over and gave her a big hug.
"Don't be sad," she said.
"I'll ring the man at the airport tomorrow."

She kissed Carla on the top of her head.
"Sleep well," she said, kindly.

But Carla didn't sleep well at all.
She tossed and turned all night.
She missed Russy and she was sure
he missed her, too!

Chapter 3
Great News

The next morning when Carla
came down for breakfast,
Nana was on the phone again.
"Oh, really!" she cried. "That is great news!"

As she put down the phone,
Nana smiled at Carla.

"What is it, Nana?" cried Carla.
"Has someone found Russy?"

"Well," replied Nana, a big smile spreading
across her face,
"your little teddy has been all the way
to Japan, and is now on his way back!
The plane you were on landed here
and then flew on to Japan.
When the pilot was leaving the plane,
she saw a furry little leg
poking out from underneath a seat."

"Did she pick him up?" asked Carla.

"Yes!" replied Nana, "and she took Russy to her hotel for the night."

"Oh," said Carla, sadly.
"Is she going to keep him for her little girl?"

"Oh, no!" said Nana.
"Russy is on his way back to you right now. Look!" she said, holding up her phone to Carla.
"The pilot sent me a photo."

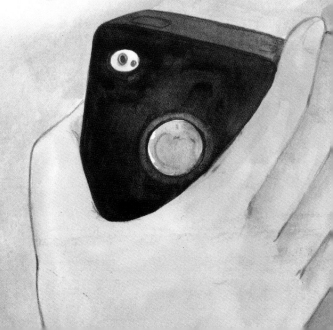

And there, on the screen, was Russy.
He was sitting right beside the pilot
in the cockpit of a large plane.

"Look!" cried Carla.
"Russy is flying the plane."

"Yes," said Nana, smiling,
"and he looks very smart in his pilot's cap."

Nana grabbed the keys to her car.
"Come on!" she said.
"Captain Russy is about to land his big plane
and he will be waiting for us at the airport!"

Chapter 4
Welcome Home

As soon as Carla and Nana
arrived at the airport,
they went straight to gate number 7.
Carla and Nana waited and waited —
until, finally, the last person came off.
"I don't think Russy is coming,"
said Carla, turning sadly to Nana.
"Maybe the pilot kept him after all."

Nana just smiled.

"Look, Carla!" she said,
turning towards gate number 7.

Carla quickly turned around.

A tall woman wearing
a blue pilot's uniform
walked towards them.

"Oh!" cried Carla. "It's Russy!"
And she ran over to her teddy.

"Welcome home, Captain Russy," said Carla.
Then she gave him the biggest hug ever!